John Edward Bullard Jewett

The genealogy of the Ball and Weston families

With a poem by Rev. J.E.B. Jewett

John Edward Bullard Jewett

The genealogy of the Ball and Weston families
With a poem by Rev. J.E.B. Jewett

ISBN/EAN: 9783337132354

Printed in Europe, USA, Canada, Australia, Japan

Cover: Foto ©Andreas Hilbeck / pixelio.de

More available books at **www.hansebooks.com**

THE GENEALOGY

OF THE

BALL AND WESTON FAMILIES,

WITH A

POEM,

BY

REV. J. E. B. JEWETT,

OF PEPPERELL, MASS.

FITCHBURG:
PRINTED AT THE SENTINEL OFFICE, 176 MAIN STREET.
1867.

THE GENEALOGY

OF THE

BALL AND WESTON FAMILIES,

WITH A

POEM,

BY

REV. J. E. B. JEWETT,

OF PEPPERELL, MASS.

FITCHBURG
PRINTED AT THE SENTINEL OFFICE, 116 MAIN STREET,
1867.

GENEALOGY

OF THE

BALL AND WESTON FAMILIES.

AT a gathering of a few families of the Balls and Westons, at the place known as the Levi Ball place, in Townsend, May 31st, 1865, it was proposed that there should be a gathering, one year from that time, at the place where Ebenezer, son of Jeremiah Ball, settled in the year 1753, and where his son Noah lived until his death, and that all who were connexions of either of the families, should be invited to attend.

Providence favored us with a pleasant day, and as the hour of nine approached, the people began to assemble, coming from far and near. There were relatives from twenty-five different towns, and from four States, viz: N. H., Vt., Mass., and R. I. The occasion was very much enlivened by music given by the Pepperell Cornet Band. After spending several hours in pleasant conversation, and welcoming many friends, who for years had been severed, and forming many new acquaintances, we were invited to seat ourselves at the table, where there were ample provisions made for all present, about three hundred. They were then invited to listen to a Poem given by Rev. J. E. B. Jewett, also, to remarks and singing by many of the relatives.

The following Hymn was read and sung, written by Mrs. B. W. Farmer of New Iberia, Louisiana. entitled

THE REUNION.

Brothers and sisters, sire and son,
Mothers and daughters fair,
Little ones wild with frolic and fun,
Toddling feet just learning to run;
Methinks it's a foretaste of Heaven begun,
Such a blessed reunion to share.

Call not the world all heartless and cold,
When pleasures like these cheer our way;
The germs of sweet friendship their beauties unfold,
The hearts thus refreshed must cease to grow old,
And the mine of affection, more precious than gold,
Love's labor will ever repay.

Ah! could I be with you, such joy it would give,
As never on earth may be mine;
It were worth half a lifetime such moments to live,
And taste such sweet pleasures as never deceive,
As the home circle gathers bright garlands to weave,
For the brow of affections divine.

Though Fate may deny me such blessings to share,
I will put all my labors away,
And bidding a truce to harassing care,
The thoughts unrestrained will be hovering there,
While I here keep your Festival day.

Mrs. Farmer was driven from her home by the Rebels and went to New Orleans for protection from our army. She soon found there were soldiers in the Twenty-sixth and Fifty-third Mass. Regiments, from her native place (Townsend) and vicinity. She became very much interested in their welfare, and administered to their wants. The acts of kindness received from herself and daughter will never be forgotten.

It was proposed that a Record of the Ball and Weston families, and also the Poem and Hymns read and sung at the gathering, be published.

THE BALL MEMORIAL.

A POEM, BY J. E. B. JEWETT.

TIME flies,—the generations come and go ;
So it has been,—it always will be so.
The Stream of time is ever flowing on,—
The years once here, are now forever gone.
Adown its current generations glide,
Then sleep in death, beneath the silent tide.
Each thirty years that run their rapid rounds,
Depopulate the earth throughout its bounds.
Each hundred years no vestige leave of men,
Who, back a hundred years, were living then.
Our Fathers, where are they ? Their race is run,—
Their lives are ended, and their labors done.
 Thus Time works wonders on our human race,
And soon will find for us our resting place.
Before its scythe the aged soon must bow,
And they will sleep, where sleep their fathers now.
Nearer each day their faltering footsteps tend,
And they, ere long, will reach their journey's end.
We, in the midst of life, must soon grow old,
Then, soon, the story of our life is told.
Those younger, soon are women and are men,—
No longer children, as they erst have been.
The child remains not long a child, but grows,— .
Anon, it's drest in men's or women's clothes.
Since some of you were boys and girls at play,
Some three-score years have sped you on your way.
But as you take a retrospective view,
These intervening years seem short and few.
And we, in middle life, can look behind,
And call the scenes of childhood all to mind,
Our lives seem like a dream when we awake,

So rapid is the progress which we make.
So fleet is Time,—our years revolve so fast,
That we forget how much of life is past.
The rapid years roll round, and they unroll,
Of human life, the transitory scroll.
And we shall find, my friends, that we are not,
At all, exceptions to the common lot—
We all do fade, as fades the leaf,—
Our days are few, our life-march is but brief—
A few more years, and life's glad scenes are past,—
That year is nigh which is to be our last.

But drop we now these grave, lackluster strains,
And let our thoughts pursue some lighter trains.
We welcome, welcome you, from far and near,
Our friends, who now are congregated here.
Sprung from one stock, or else by wedlock, all
Claim some connexion with the name of Ball.
Some here are Balls by blood, and some by name,
And some by marriage-ties, but's all the same;
We claim an interest in the parent tree,
Whate'er our name or our relation be.

As generations come, and as they go,
Names strangely change as well as things, you know.
Our daughters so esteem the other sex,
That most of them do not withhold their necks,
But choose to take on Hymen's yoke for life,
Than not to be, what they desire—a wife.
So strong and deep their interest in mankind,
That they sometimes will even "go it blind."
Urged on, mayhap, by cunning Cupid's dart,
They wish for union—not to "mourn apart."
Though they succeed and seem to win the game,
They give up all, withholding not their name.
They sacrifice their names,—too, their effects,
And take the sir-name of the other sex.
'Tis queer what they won't do, and what their plans
To swop their maiden-names and take a man's.
'Tis thus it comes about, as in this case,
That names are no criterion of our race;
Our names are lost, but not our pedigree,
We still are branches of the Balline tree.

We, then, who claim relationship, are here—
For what intent, I trust will soon appear.
If 'tis to have a *ball* and frolicin',
"The light, fantastic toe" and violin,
With the concomitants, I feel chagrin,
And must confess that I am " taken in."
If 'tis to be a ball like those of old,
I will " give in" that I am fairly " sold."
" Skedaddle" let us, taking to our heels
Across these pastures, woodlots and these fields.
Guess that I should not fiddle if I could,
And, " what's the matter," could not if I would.
It may, maybe, be so with all of us;
If so, our dance would turn out in a muss.
And so, should you require of me to dance,
I reckon I should not accept the chance.
No doubt our elder uncles and our aunts
Are more familiar with this ordinance;
Who, though they learnt some fifty years ago,
Could show us how they used to "jump Jim Crow."
And yet, for one, I should not care to see
Their wanton waltzing and hilarity.
And with respect to merry-making drink,
Which balls require, (as dancers mostly think,)
Their limbs to limber, and their souls to cheer,
Don't think we've got a single bottle here.
And what is more, 'twould be a sorry sight,
To trip fantastic here in broad daylight.
'Tis said somewhere, " There is a time to dance;"
That this is not, we see it at a glance.
And more, we should account it a disgrace,
To play our pranks at such a time and place.
   It must be then, for some more wise intent,
That we are here, who are of Ball descent.
What this intent may be I can't divine,
But to some such opinions I incline,—
Perhaps it is to see what sort of folks we are,
And how with other people we compare;
Perhaps it is to show an honest pride
That we have so " increased and multiplied;"

Or, p'raps, that we, the members of this race,
Should meet and greet each other face to face,
And all as one, with a becoming grace,
Pay our regards to this ancestral place.

   Is this the purpose then, for which we've met,
'Tis one we have no reason to regret.
'Tis meet that those of " kith and kin" should feel
A common interest in each other's weal.
'Tis meet that we, with filial steps should trace,
The precincts of this patriarchal place ;
And here commune, upon this cherished spot,
Where our great parents lived—but now " are not."
Right here, in days of yore, as man and wife,
They pitched their tent and settled down for life.
Here they their mutual joys and sorrows shared ;
Here loved, and here for life and death prepared.
'Twas here our grandsire, in those bygone years,
Yoked up and drove afield, his wain and steers ;
Here felled the forest trees and tilled the soil,
And earned his daily bread with patient toil.
'Twas here, broadcast, his grain he used to sow ;
Here he his broom-corn raised, and here his flax,
And money to defray his yearly tax.
And here it was, upon this very hill,
His sacks with rye and corn he used to fill,
And then would horseback them away to mill.
Here lowed his kine and made these hills resound ;
And here his bellowing oxen pawed the ground.
Here grazed his sheep, and wolves disturbed their peace,
And cunning foxes stole his screaming geese.

   Here Grandam Ball stood at her spinning wheel,
And here she wound her yarn around her reel.
Here stood her loom, that wonderful machine,
Which now is out of vogue, or seldom seen.
Here she, with busy feet, the treadle plied,
And now the straggling thrums she stopt and tied,
Then forth and back the flying shuttle drove
Athwart the warp, and so her cloth she wove.

   'Twas here she reared her numerous little fold,
And fed them porridge, " best when nine days old ;"

And them she clad with homespun which she made,
Indebted to her dye-pot for its shade.
The Decalogue she taught them all to say,
Each week, at nightfall of the Sabbath-day.
Here lay the Bible out of which was taught,
Those lessons which these children ne'er forgot.
This was almost their only book,—and this,
Their guiding star, conducted them to bliss.
Indeed, this is a hallowed spot to us,
And let us all as one regard it thus.
For prayers here said, are bringing blessings still
On us, who now our parents' places fill.
The lives they lived revert in good to all
Descended from our great grand-parents—Ball.

Descendants of our ancient, honored sires,
Survive there still in us their wonted fires ?
The virtues which were theirs do we retain ?
Or, do we look for them, and look in vain ?
If I mistake not—taken all in all,—
We do fair justice to the name of Ball.
As children rise, and take the fathers' place,
They do not shame,—reproach them, and disgrace.
Renowned and great I know that we are not,
And this may never be our children's lot.
I know we have not set the world a-blaze,—
Sailed round the world, or walked the "starry ways."
We cannot boast of great celebrities,—
We have no nonpareils, or prodigies,
We did not give the world the " iron horse ;"
Nor can we boast of a Professor Morse.
To great reforms we have not given birth,
Nor have we revolutionized the earth.
And yet, we have our geniuses and lights,
Who have, or mean to have, their patent rights.
In what are termed the lib'ral, learned professions,
We have not made tremendous marked, impressions.
Still, some of us do practice, also preach ;
And some are squires, and some do sometimes teach.
We've raised no Presidents, or Governors,—
Nor Gen'rl Grants, to wage our civil wars.

Perhaps the country would be more content,
Had politicians blown for us, and spent
Their time and breath, and, as a consequent,
Made one of us its *present* President.

And yet, though we have made so little stir,
Nor great sensations made, like Aaron Burr,—
We are not drones or useless cyphers here,
As from our private records will appear.
The world is better off with us, no doubt,
Be what we may, than it would be without;
And this, I 'spose, is more than we could say
Of some whole races, at the present day.

We have an offset to our lack of fame,—
For, as a race, we've earned a worthy name.
We are respected, and deserve respect,
Despite our faults which others may detect.
We are not poor, nor "*visa versa*," rich,
Which Agur would not be, no matter which.
Industrious, temp'rate, labor-loving folks,
Our frames are ample, and as tough as oaks.
" A feeble folk," 'tis said, the conies are ;—
Robuster folk than we are found nowhere.
We live by labor, and by labor thrive,—
Have force and "grit" enough, and are alive.
We " hoe our row," as through the world we go,
Be what our station may, one high or low.
The almshouse finds us not its sorry guests,
Nor are we renegades and public pests.
Some men depend upon their wits, but we,
More on our muscles, and our industry.

'Tis true, nor should I keep it out of sight,—
We are an honest race, and love the right.
Good, law-abiding, law-sustaining men
We are ; and such those gone before have been.
In games and tricks, intrigues, and what is mean,
We are not found,—at least, are seldom seen :
Nor are we found, as our own record tells,
In lockups, jails, and dreary prison-cells.

We have our idiosyncrasies, I know,—
But what of that? with others 'tis just so.

Peculiarities are bad enough.
But after all, they a'nt the worst of stuff.
We are not odd—so odd as some we see,
Still, some are odder some than's best to be.

As to our looks, compared to other races,
We differ some, still we have human faces.
We claim, our " port and bearing" will compare,
With that of people almost anywhere.
At least, I wot, our looks are no disgrace,
To any people of the Yankee race.
Should our deportment tally with our mein,
We need not worry at our being seen.
We have no features, hues, or quirks, or crooks,
Which much disfigure us, or mar our looks.
That we may better cut our way along,   [strong,—
Through " thick and thin," and through resistance
And better overcome whate'er opposes,
And better sniff the breeze, and scent of roses—
We, as a gen'ral thing, have gen'rous noses.
Our looks are such, our market price is fair
As other people's market prices are.
We find, in fact, we are in such demand,
We get, (if wished,) another's heart and hand.
In fine, our looks are such, or such our lives,
That we secure good husbands, and *fair** wives.
Still, I advise to all, both old and young,
Don't feel concerned about your " being hung,"
(Some folks, 'tis said, are plagued and pestered thus,
And get into a hubbub and a muss—;)
And guard against it, as your bounden duty—
Because of your supposed angelic *beauty.*

Although akin, respecting politics,
We may belong to disagreeing cliques.
We have a right, I know, to disagree,
And let us do it right, and honestly.
All cannot think alike, and cannot be ;—
And so we will agree to disagree.
If we are wrong, let's try to find it out,
And when we are convinced, face right about.

*One of the most accommodating words in the language.

Injustice would be done, as I suppose,
Did I not simply add, before I close,
That ours is a religious race of men,
With rather rare exceptions now and then.
Those gone before were mostly men of prayer,
And most who follow them, their virtues share.
They took as theirs, nor did they set at naught
The Faith the Master and Apostles taught.
Our fathers' child-like faith let us embrace,
And all our heirs be heirs of saving grace.
The faith they walked by led them up to God,—
Let us pursue the path our fathers trod.
It was to them—will be to us, a stay,
Which neither life nor death can take away.
    Kindred and Friends,—bound by a common tie,
And heirs of those whose record is on high—
Good men and true ;—'tis ours to emulate,
What in our sires was worthy, good and great.
It is a satisfaction to us all,
To own the name and pedigree of Ball ;
It is an honor and our pride to be
Descendants of so good an ancestry.
'Tis ours to represent this worthy race,
And save the name that's left us from disgrace.
Its ancient virtues,—may they still abound,—
And we grow more, not less and less, renowned ;
And so transmit these virtues down the tide,
On which the nascent generations glide.
By building up ourselves in what is good,—
By seeking help, whence help alone can come,
And living mindful of our future home,—
We thus, and thus alone, shall best fulfill
Our mission here, and too, Jehovah's will.
Our fathers' God let each of us revere,
And honor Him, while we continue here.
So when, like theirs, our pilgrimage is o'er,
And we, as they, have reached the other shore,
Those following us shall meet, with honest pride,
And say : " 'Twas here my parents lived and died."

HYMN.

The following closing Hymn, written by H. N. Spaulding,
was then sung:

Now is o'er this time of meeting,
Ended is our festive day;
Did we bring a cordial greeting?
Have we found a blessing—say?
Friends and kindred,
Have we found a blessing—say?

Oh! how memory's tide has borne us
To the scenes of other years,
When this cherished spot resounded
With loved voices—hushed in tears;
They have left us,
Gone beyond earth's hopes and fears.

Oh, thou God of all the living,
Hear our cry for those that stay;
May each sin-sick soul be breathing,
Lord, we perish—save to-day;
Great Physician,
Speed thy work without delay.

Then may all our names be entered,
In that book of endless life,
Each endearing tie unsevered,
Strengthen'd still with beauty rife.
Happy meeting
With the pure in endless life.

GENEALOGICAL RECORD.

John Ball came from Wiltshire, England, to Concord, Mass., in the year 1640, and died Oct. 1st, 1655. Nathaniel, his son, was about ten years old when his father settled in Concord, about three-fourths of a mile east of the meeting-house. Nathaniel had four sons, viz: Ebenezer, Eleazer, John and Nathaniel.

Nathaniel the 2d, had seven sons, viz: Caleb, Nathaniel, Thomas, James, Jeremiah, Benjamin and Ebenezer.

Jeremiah, the son of Nathaniel the 2d, came to Townsend, Mass., and settled in the east part of the town, near the house where Jonas Spaulding now lives, in the year 1726. He married Mary Stevens, 1727. He died April 12th, 1780, aged 79 years. She died Feb. 11th, 1764, aged 62 years; they had six children.

1. Ebenezer, the third male child, born in Townsend, July 3d, 1729, married Rebecca Butterfield, of Westford, 1753. He died April 7th, 1797, aged 68 years. She was born July 31st, 1729, and died Oct. 21st, 1800, aged 72 years.

2. Lieut. Jeremiah, born Aug. 31st, 1731, married Mary Stevens, of Townsend, Jan., 1759, and died March 7th, 1792. She was born March 11th, 1739, and died May 3d, 1825.

3. Mary, born June 24th, 1733, married three husbands, viz: Hubbard, Baldwin, and Jedediah Jewett. She died Aug. 11th, 1822.

4. Elizabeth, born March 4th, 1736.

5. Susannah, born March 11th, 1738, married Dutton.

6. Benjamin, born July 26th, 1742, and settled in Hancock, N. H.

THE CHILDREN OF EBENEZER AND REBECCA BALL.

1. Rebecca, b. Nov. 8th, 1754, m. 1st, Feb. 20th, 1787.
Wm. Weston of Townsend, b. Feb. 9th, 1744, d. Oct. 15th.
1819, aged 75. She m. 2d, Abel Keyes of Townsend, Mass.
She m. 3d, April 27th, 1830, Rogers Weston of Mason, N. H..
b. Sept. 30th, 1757, d. March 9th, 1843, aged 86. She d.
August 15th, 1830, aged 76.

2. Ebenezer Ball, b. Sept. 2d, 1756, m. Oct. 18th, 1781,
Sarah Shattuck of Pepperell, b. Sept. 3d, 1755, d. July 8th,
1785, aged 30 ; m. 2d, June, 1786, Hannah Smith of Mason,
N. H. She d. April 4th, 1787. He m. 3d, Oct. 10th, 1787,
Phebe Weston of Townsend, b. Dec. 19th, 1767, d. Nov. 2d,
1848, aged 81. He d. Dec. 5th, 1837, aged 81.

3. Olive Ball, b. Sept. 6th, 1758, m. Nov. 11th, 1784.
John Blood of Pepperell, b. April 15th, 1761, d. April 27th,
1833, aged 72. She d. Dec. 5th, 1838, aged 80.

4. Susannah Ball, b. Oct. 22d, 1760, m. Dec. 16th, 1788.
Joseph Heywood of Chelmsford, b. April 10th, 1761, d. Sept.
5th, 1805, aged 45. She d. Oct. 9th, 1833, aged 73.

5. Hannah Ball, b. Oct. 20th, 1762, m. Mar. 22d, 1786,
Nathaniel Shattuck of Pepperell, b. Jan. 5th, 1764, d. June
14th, 1847, aged 83. She d. June 5th, 1833, aged 70.

6. Abraham Ball, b. Jan. 26th, 1765, m. 1785, Deliverance
Perham of Westford, b. April 20th, 1765, d. Dec. 29th, 1838,
aged 73. He d. Sept. 15th, 1840, aged 75.

7. Bathsheba Ball, b. June 14th, 1769, m. Nov. 16th, 1791,
Hezekiah Winn of Chelmsford, b. April 27th, 1768, d. Dec.
23d, 1855, aged 87. She d. May 2d, 1815, aged 46.

8. Noah Ball, b. Aug. 3d, 1771, m. May 26th, 1796, Betsey
Weston of Townsend, b. Feb. 29th, 1775, d. Sept. 16th, 1843,
aged 68. He d. Aug. 28th, 1847, aged 76.

9. Mary Ball, b. May 6th, 1773, m. December 20th, 1797,
Zaccheus Richardson of Townsend, b. Jan. 21, 1771, d. March
5th, 1860, aged 89. She d. Mar. 6th, 1858, aged 85.

REBECCA BALL'S DESCENDANTS BY WM. WESTON.

1. Lucy Weston, b. Mar. 11th, 1789, m. Samuel Rockwood of Groton, Mar., 1840. She d. Apr. 1843; no issue.

2. Wm. Weston, b. Mar. 1st, 1791, m. Oct. 24th, 1816, Dolly Hodgman of Ashby. He d. Aug. 18th, 1866, and had 1st, Clarissa, b. Mar. 6th, 1818, d. Sept. 28th, 1819. 2d, Charles, b. June 8th, 1819, d. July 15th, 1858. 3d, Harriet, b. Oct. 27th, 1822, m. Apr. 1st, 1841, Nero Sherwin of Townsend; had two children who died. 4th. Wm. b. Jan. 4th, 1825, m. Nov. 30th, 1848, Harriet Emery of Lunenburg. She was b. May 23d, 1828, and has one child, Lizzie M. Weston, b. Aug. 22d, 1   . 5th, Elizabeth, b. Sept. 4th, 1827, d. Nov. 10th, 1837.

3. Sarah Weston, b. Sept. 18th, 1794, m. May 9th, 1820, John Hodgman of Townsend, b. March 21st, 1794. She d. Dec. 10th, 1838. He d. Jan. 21st, 1853, and had, 1st, Mary Hodgman, b. Nov. 19th, 1823, m. George Gassett and lives at the West, and has children. 2d, Wm., b. April 3d, 1821, d. Nov. 10th, 1839. 3d, Elnathan, b. April 23d, 1826, m. and had children; d. in the war. 4th, Rodney, b. Nov. 1st, 1828, m. 1866, Hannah Otis of Townsend. 5th, Celista, b. Dec. 7th, 1830, m. George Shipley of Nashua, N. H. 6th, Lucy, b. July 29th, 1835, d. in Townsend, August 11th, 1864. 7th, Sarah, b. May 9th, 1838, d. Sept. 13th, 1838.

EBENEZER BALL'S DESCENDANTS.

1. Sarah Ball, b. Nov. 20th, 1782, m. Nov. 3d, 1808, Deacon Samuel Walker of Townsend. He was b. Mar. 27th, 1783, d. July 19th, 1859. She d. Jan. 3d, 1854, and had, 1st, Samuel H. Walker, b. Nov. 13th, 1809, d. Jan. 6th, 1824. 2d, Lucy B., b. Aug. 22d, 1811, d. July 5th, 1813. 3d, John, b. May 13th, 1816, m. Lydia Adams of Townsend, and had, 1st, Francis M., 2d, Elisabeth M., 3d, Annette, 4th, Martha, 5th, John Q. A., 6th, Mary E., 7th, Clara, and 8th, Edna. 4th, Levi, b. Feb. 5th, 1816, m. Lydia Walker of Union, Me., and had, 1st,

Augusta M., 2d, Ruhamah A., 3d, Albina M., 4th, Myra D. and 5th, Martha. 5th, Sarah S., b. Dec. 18th, 1818, m. June 17th, 1838, Wm. Ball of Chicopee. She d. May 19th, 1849; had, 1st, Albina S. Ball, 2d, George W., 3d, Edwin P. 6th, Nathan, b. Feb. 19th, 1832, m. Elizabeth Worcester of Ashby; had, 1st, Edward H., 2d, Sarah, 3d, Ellen. 7th, Hannah, b. July 10th, 1824, m. Daniel D. Smith of Townsend; had, 1st, Alden W. Smith, b. March 18th, 1845, 2d, Estella R., b. Oct. 2d, 1847, 3d, Sarah C., b. July 19th, 1849, d. Aug. 25th, 1850, 4th, Mary A., b. Dec. 26th, 1851, 5th, Charles F., b. Dec. 5th, 1854, 6th, Arthur F., b. May 15th, 1856.

2. Ebenezer Ball, b. April 2d, 1767, m. Sarah Swift of Ware. He d. Dec. 31st, 1845; had 1st, William, b. May 7th, 1815, 2d, Emory, b. Sept. 11th, 1818, 3d, Amos, b. June 14th, 1820, d. Aug. 1846, 4th, Hosea, b. Sept. 20th, 1822, 5th, Mary Mariva, b. Dec. 29th, 1825.

3. David Ball, b. Nov. 7th, 1788, m. Nancy Weston of North Reading. He d. Mar. 1863; had no issue.

4. Deacon Levi Ball, b. July 7th, 1790, m. Jan. 10th, 1813, Lucy Burbank of Harvard, b. July 16th, 1787, in Harvard. He d. Oct. 11th, 1849. She d. Oct. 7th, 1848; they had 1st, Lucy Ball, b. Aug. 30th, 1814, d. Sept. 10th, 1814, 2d, Lucy B. Ball, b. Oct. 18th, 1815, d. June 7th, 1832, 3d, Harriet N. Ball, b. Apr. 25th, 1817, m. Lucius F. Woods of Leominster. She d. May 23d, 1860, and had, 1st, Francena Wood. m. David Haselton of West Townsend, 2d, Francis W. Wood, 4th and 5th, Caleb Walton and Levi Warren, b. May 26th, 1818, Warren, m. Lucy A. Coffin of. Wisconsin, Oct. 1862; they have Mary W., b. Jan. 1st, 1866. Lucy A., wife of Warren Ball, d. Aug. 1866, in Brothers-Town, Wisconsin.

Hervey Ball, b. April 21st, 1820, m. Nov. 23d, 1848, Ann S. Tucker, b. Aug. 17th, 1826, in Pepperell. They have, 1st, Anna C., b. June 28th, 1854; 2d, Frederick H., b. Oct. 27th, 1854; 3d, Hattie N., b. May 1st, 1860; Samuel W., b. Feb. 14th, 1863, in Brothers-Town, Wis.

Mary W. Ball, b. July 13th, 1822, m. 1st, Samuel P. Barrett, Dec. 1st, 1846. He d. Sept. 27th, 1847. She m. 2d, Jan. 10th, 1850, Merrick Phelps, 'and had George W. B. Phelps.

Abbie Ball, b. Oct. 25th, 1823, m. Nov. 23d, 1852, Moses Barrett of Lancaster. He d. July 20th, 1858. She d. June 13th, 1863. They had, 1st, Herbert M., b. Jan. 31st, 1855 ; 2d, Arthur C., b. Jan. 27th, 1856 ; 3d, Mary A., b. Mar. 22d, 1858.

Eliza Jane Ball, b. June 22d, 1826, d. Aug. 29th, 1826.

5. Rev. Hosea Ball, b. Aug. 11th, 1792, m. Sept. 12th, 1817, Sarah Helmes of Monroe, Orange Co., N. Y. ; had 1st & 2d, twins b. July 3d, 1819, d. July 4th, 1819 ; 3d, Luther H. Ball, b. Oct. 10th, 1820, son of Hosea, who was the son of Ebenezer, who was the son of Ebenezer, who was the son of Jeremiah, who was the son of Nathaniel, who was the son of Nathaniel, who was the son of John, who came from Wiltshire, England, and settled in Concord, Mass., m. Elizabeth Vail of Monroe, by whom he had two children ; 1st, Mary Isabel, 2d, Eleanor J. She d. May 1st, 1846. He m. 2d, Phebe Garrison of Warwick, July 4th, 1848, by whom he had, 3d, George H., 4th, Sarah Ann, d., 5th, Garrison J., 6th, Charles H., 7th, John F., 8th, Paulina A., 9th, Harriet A., 10th, David B., 11th, Luther H. 4th, Harriet N., b. Mar. 21st, 1823, m. Samuel A. Heath, formerly of Bradford, Mass., by whom she had George L. and Ida N. She d. Feb. 11th, 1861. 5th, Catherine E., b. May 16th, 1826, m. Samuel E. Tucker of Pepperell, by whom she had, 1st, Charles A., 2d, Clarence C., 3d, Alice M. 4th, Mary E., 5th, Sarah, 6th, Varnum E. Ball, b. Jan. 17th, 1829, d. Mar. 15th, 1844 ; 7th, Eleanor J., born Nov. 12th, 1832, m. Samuel Smith of Munroe, by whom she had, 1st, Charles, 2d, Sarah J., 3d, John W., 4th, Andrew, 5th, Lydia, 6th, Levi, 8th, Mary R., b. Dec. 10th, 1834, m. Sept. 7th, 1866, Daniel Green of Munroe, N. Y., 9th, Paulina V., b. Aug. 17th, 1838, m. Aug. 20th, 1864, David B. Burbank of Lancaster, Mass., and settled in Tomales, California.

6. Phebe Ball, born August 4th, 1794, m. Dec. 31st, 1833,

Captain Edmund Blood of Pepperell, b. July 5th, 1764, by whom she had Edmund Harvey Newton Blood, b. April 13th, 1835, m. June 11th, 1867, Mary Anna Fletcher of Hollis, N. H., b. April 9th, 1841. She d. July 31st, 1852. He d. Nov. 16th, 1843.

7. Samuel Ball, b. August 7th, 1796, m. Olive Nelson of Stafford, Conn., by whom he had, 1st, George Ball, 2d, Hannah Ball, 3d, Samuel E. Ball, 4th, Alvin Ball.

8. Hannah Ball, b. Oct. 31st, 1800, m. Oct. 10th, 1821, Samuel W. Burbank of Lancaster. She d. Feb. 17th, 1840, by whom she had, 1st, Susan E. Burbank, b. Sept. 2d, 1822, d. July 20th, 1825, 2d, Sarah M., b. Feb. 21st, 1826, m. Nov. 1846, A. F. Kidder of Lancaster, by whom she had, 1st, Marcia L. Kidder, 2d, Lizzie Kidder. Parents now dead. 3d, Hannah E., b. April 5th, 1828, d. March 23d, 1843, 4th, George W., b. Nov. 17th, 1829, m. Apphie R. Blake ; settled in California ; 5th, Lucy A., b. April 4th, 1831, d. May 29th, 1848 ; 6th, Hosea H., b. Oct. 13th, 1834, m. Nov., 1860, E. H. Anderson, and had one son, Henry ; 7th, Eliza J., b. April 17th, 1836, m. George V. Ball, March 3d, 1864 ; 8th, David B., b. August 6th, 1838, m. P. V. Ball, August 20th, 1864.

9. Roxanna Ball, b. Nov. 23d, 1804, m. Dec. 10th, 1834, Nathan Davis of Acton, by whom she had, 1st, Sarah E., b. Sept. 22d, 1835, d. 1836, 2d, Harriet E., b. March 16th, 1837, 3d, Hannah A., b. August 12th, 1840, d. May 10th, 1842, 4th, Hannah E., b. Sept. 24th, 1844, m. Oct. 5th, 1862, Edward Walker of Townsend, by whom she had Edward E. Walker.

10. Varnum Ball, b. June 30th, 1807, m., Sept. 2d, 1828, Nancy Ball of Lunenburg. She was b. Jan. 13th, 1796 ; they had, 1st, Phebe Ann Ball, b. Dec. 9th, 1832, m. August 27th, 1854, Lorrell Holman of Lunenburg ; they have, 1st, George Lord, d ; 2d, Edith A. 2. George V. Ball, b. June 25th, 1844, m. March 3d, 1864, Eliza J. Burbank of Lancaster, b. April 17th, 1836 ; they have Varnum W., and have settled in California. Varnum Ball has buried three infants.

OLIVE .BALL'S DESCENDANTS BY JOHN BLOOD.

1. John Blood, b. August 2d, 1785, m. May 2d, 1812, Susan Jewett of Pepperell, b. Dec. 3d, 1786, d. May 16th, 1856. He d. April 11th, 1850; they had, 1st, Susan M., b. Feb. 17th, 1813, m. March 18th, 1845, Columbus Eames of Northborough, and **ad,** 1st, John A., 2d, Ellen M. 2. John E. Blood, b. May 1st, 1815, m. Feb. 6th, 1849, Mary E. D. Bancroft of Fitchburg; had, 1st, Nellie E., 2d, John II., 3d, M. Florence E. 3. Henry II. Blood, b. June 11th, 1817. 4. L. Jane Blood, b. Feb. 11th, 1820, m. Dec. 28th, 1857, Eli Boynton of Pepperell; has no issue. 5. Andrew J. Blood, b. August 7th, 1822. d. in California, Sept. 15th, 1850. 6. James II. Blood, b. Jan. 16th, 1825.

2. Noah Blood, b. July 20th, 1787, m. Dec. 4th, 1816, Hannah P. Chase of Millbury. She was b. March 27th, 1795. He d. Feb. 17th, 1850; they had, 1st, Noah O. Blood, b. Oct. 3d, 1819, m. Oct., 1845, Evelyn W. Burgess of Concord; they have, 1st, Eva C., 2d, Mary A., 3d, Willie O. 2. Lorenzo P. Blood, b. July 25th, 1824, m. Nov. 1855, Margaret G. Thomson of Marblehead; they have, 1st, Samuel T., 2d, Annah P., 3d, Margaret G.

3. Olive Blood, b. April 13th, 1791, d. June 18th, 1795.

4. Rebecca Blood, b. April 25th, 1793, m. Dec. 3d, 1817, Deacon Henry Jewett of Pepperell. He was b. Oct. 28th, 1792; they had, 1st, Henry A. Jewett, b. Jan. 14th, 1820, m. May 21st, 1849, Sarah Lawrence of Hampton, and settled in Northborough as a physician, and has, 1st, Henry A, 2d, Annah R., 3d, Flassie L. 2. John E. B. Jewett, b. Dec. 9th, 1821, m. 1st, Feb. 12th 1851, Sophronia Wilson of New Ipswich, N. H.; m. 2d, Jan. 10th, 1854, Frances II. Lacy of Jaffrey, N. H., and was settled in Jaffrey as a Gospel minister, Sept. 25th, 1851, and now lives in Pepperell; they have, 1st, Mary M., b. March 15th, 1857, 2d, Martha F., b. Jan. 27th, 1859, d. Dec. 9th, 1860, 3d, Ella F., b. July 4th, 1862. 3. Frederic A. Jewett, b. Sept. 6th, 1824, m. June 1st, 1854, Harriet C. Torrey of Weymouth; they have, 1st, Harriet R., 2d, Frederic,

d. ; 3d Alice, and settled in Shrewsbury, Mass. as a physician. 4. Charles F. Jewett, b. May 28th, 1828, m. August 26th, 1855, Georgie S. Loring of Pepperell, and have, 1st, Franklin G., 2d, Charles II., 3d, Edward S., 4th, Edith Rebecca. 5. Rebecca M. Jewett, b. Sept. 19th, 1830, m. July 9th, 1851, Philo B. Wilcox, d. April 1st, 1852.

SUSANNAH BALL'S DESCENDANTS BY JOS. HEYWOOD.

1. Susannah Heywood, b. Sept. 30th, 1789, m. John Chamberlain of Grand Isle on Lake Champlain.

2. Betsey Heywood, b. Nov. 6th, 1790, m. 1st, Oct. 21st, 1819, John Wright of Westford, d.; they have John F. Wright, b. Oct. 14th, 1821, m. Oct. 1843, Lavinia Frye of Lowell ; had four children. 2d, m. Benjamin Heywood of Jaffrey, N. H., Dec. 7th, 1843 ; had no issue. d.

3. Joseph Heywood, b. in Chelmsford, June 4th, 1792, m. Sept. 10th, 1819, Fidelia Reed, b. July 20th, 1793, in Westford ; they had, 1st, Joseph E. Heywood, b. Jan. 21st, 1821, m. 2d, John S. Heywood, b. Oct. 6th, 1822, m. and had children. 3d. Elizabeth Heywood, b. March 10th, 1825. 4th, Isaac B. Heywood, b. March 1st, 1828, m. —— Smith. 5th Susan M. Heywood, b. Jan. 14th, 1830. 6th, Charles Heywood, b. Jan. 20th, 1833, m. Isabel Keyes ; they had one child. 7th. Mary E. Heywood, b. July 29th, 1835, m. Charles Sampson, removed out West. 8th, Ann L. Heywood, b. June 14th, 1837.

4. Hannah Heywood, b. Sept. 14th 1793, m. 1814, Isaac Bancroft of Lowell. He was b. 1790. She d. Sept. 7th, 1853, and had, 1st, Hannah E. Bancroft, d. Aug. 2d, 1866. 2d, Lucy Bancroft, m. —— Stevens, of Fitchburg, and d. Dec. 12th, 1856, and had Lucy E. Stevens. 3d, Edward J. Bancroft, is m. and lives in Montreal, Canada, and has had four children.

5. Polly Heywood, b. May 14th, 1796, m. 1823, Stowell Bancroft of Groton, d. Jan. 3d, 1825 ; had one child, Mary Bancroft, b. Dec., 1824, m. —— Hardy of Lowell.

6. Benjamin Heywood, b. April 30th, 1798, m. Feb. 29th, 1833, Esther Richardson of Townsend. He d. June 10th, 1862; they had, 1st, Julia Heywood, b. Dec. 7th, 1834, m. Albert Richardson of California; they have two children. 2d, Benjamin, b. Jan. 13th, d. Jan. 15th, 1836. 3d, Rufus B., b. Oct. 1st, 1839. 4th, Adelia E., b. Jan. 7th, 1844. 5th, Emeline M., b. Jan. 27th, 1848. 6th, Herman F., b. Sept. 29th, 1849. 7th, Sarah Heywood, b. Dec. 27th, 1799, d. Feb. 17th, 1837.

HANNAH BALL'S DESCENDANTS BY NATHANIEL SHATTUCK OF PEPPERELL.

1. Hannah Shattuck, b. Oct. 29th, 1788, d. unm., April 30th, 1811, of the dropsy. During the last four years of her life she was tapped thirty-four times and had six hundred fifty pounds of water drawn from her side.

2. Betsy Shattuck, b. Aug. 12th, 1790, m. Nov. 17th, 1808, Rolan Shattuck of Pepperell. She d. at Greenbush, N. Y., August 9th, 1823. He d. March 11th, 1842, in N. Y.; they had, 1st, Mindwell Shattuck, b. Feb. 27th, 1809, m. Nov. 29th, 1827, Nathan Blood of Pepperell. He d. March 16th, 1862; they have, 1st, Edward A., m. Oct. 23d, 1856, Sarah J. Boynton of Pepperell; they have Willie E., 2d, Rebecca A., m. Feb. 4th, 1851, James D. Andrews, of Pepperell, and have Elmer M., Edward E., and Jonas E.; 3d, Nathan Avander, m. June 4th, 1862, Caroline M. Sawtelle of Hollis, N. H., and have Freddie A.; 4th, Ann Maria, m. Dec. 14th, 1863, Albert A..Pelton of Leominster and d. June 10th, 1866. 2d, Hannah Shattuck, b. March 7th, 1811, m. Dec. 1st, 1832, Edward F. Blood of Pepperell, and have, 1st, H. Melissa, m. Sept. 16th, 1862, Newton Elliott of Mason; they have, Etta M. and Edward A. 2d, Lovina J.. 3d, E. Alonzo, 4th, Lyman C. 3d, Simon S. Shattuck, b. Jan. 27th, 1813, m. L. C. P. Butterfield of Pepperell. She d.; m. 2d, Betsy W. Green of Brookline, N. H. He d. August 26th, 1858; they had, 1st, Simon A., d. Oct. 3d, 1847; 2d, Harlan Page, d. Jan. 9th, 1862, aged 13.

4th, Eliza Shattuck, b. March 24th, 1815, m. March, 1839, Walter Warner of Townsend, and have, 1st, Charles R. F.; 2d, Melora H. E. m. Sept. 27th, 1864, Wm. H. Woodward of Townsend, and have Charles H. and George W. 5th, Rebecca Shattuck, b. Jan. 13th, 1818, m. Sept. 4th, 1838, John Williams of Pepperell; no issue. 6th and 7th, Jonas and Ann Shattuck, twins, b. Nov. 21st, 1820, Jonas Shattuck m. May 1st, 1845, Mary J. Chapman of Pepperell; they had, 1st, Everett F., b. July 12th, 1847, d. Sept. 29th, 1865, aged 18; 2d, Ella E.; 3d, Clara M. Ann Shattuck, b. Nov. 1st, 1820, m. Oct. 4th, 1843, Daniel Blood, 2d of Pepperell, and have Rolan H., Clara A. 8th and 9th, Caroline and Adaline, twins, b. July 28th, 1823. Caroline d. August 17th, 1823. Adaline d. August 10th, 1823 in Greenbush, N. Y.

3. Nathaniel Shattuck, Esq., b. Oct. 5th, 1792, m. Dec. 30th, 1812, Betsy Green of Pepperell, and d. Nov. 23d, 1863. She d. Jan. 9th, 1855; they had, 1st, Nathaniel V. Shattuck, b. June 5th, 1813, d. Oct. 14th, 1847. 2d, Eliab B. Shattuck, b. May 15th, 1817, m. Nov. 30th, 1843, Indiana Spaulding of Townsend, and have, Orin V. 3d, Nathaniel V. Shattuck, b. May 26th, 1819, d. June 4th, 1825. 4th, Thirza Ann, b. July 21st, 1821, d. Aug. 30th, 1825. 5th, Fernando Shattuck, b. July 1st, 1823, m. Nov. 25th, 1851, Charlotte F. Gould of New Ipswich, N. H.; have had, 1st, Rinaldo C., d. May 2d, 1854; 2d, Eldorus C.; 3d, Myrtie L. and Minnie E. 6th, Augusta C. Shattuck, b. Sept. 12th, 1825, m. 1st, Sept. 12th, 1843, Abraham Lawrence of Pepperell, he d. June 16th, 1854; they had Hattie C., and Arthur E.; m. 2d, Nov. 26th, 1863, Samuel K. Blood of Shirley. 7th, Betsy Ann Caroline Shattuck, b. Jan. 3d, 1828, d. Dec. 26th, 1854. 8th, Charles E. Shattuck, b. May 6th, 1830, m. Oct. 24th, 1854, Elizabeth N. Shattuck of Pepperell, and had one child.

4. Gardner Shattuck, b. March 5th, 1795, m. Dec. 11th, 1817, Silence Warren of Ashby. She was b. Nov. 30th, 1788. He d. Sept. 18th, 1854; they had, 1st, Wm. G. Shattuck, b. May 14th, 1819, m. April 5th, 1841, Harriet B. Dyer of

Townsend, and have had, 1st, Henry G. b. Feb. 19th, 1842,
m. Sept., 1862, Laura Blood of Mason, N. H., and had, Jennie
Adela, b. August 22d, 1864; 2d, Caroline Augusta, b. April
12th. 1843; 3d, Wm. Herman, b. June 30th, 1844; 4th,
Joseph Chapman, b. Nov. 25th, 1846; 5th, Mary Elizabeth, b.
March 26th, 1848; 6th, George Francis, b. Oct, 8th, 1851;
7th, John Pollard, b. August 8th, 1855; 8th, Warren Dyer, b.
Nov. 4th, 1857. 2d, Samuel W. Shattuck, b. August 9th,
1821, m. March 14th, 1843, Sarah Ann Hartwell of Townsend. She was b. August 26th, 1822, d. Oct. 20th, 1857, and
have had, 1st, Emily, b. April 2d, 1843, d. Oct. 3d, 1857;
2d, Sarah, b. June 10th, 1845, d. May 3d, 1850; 3d, Warren, b. March 29th, 1847, d. Sept. 7th, 1849; 4th, Ned, b. October 18th, 1849; 5th, Herman, b. Jan. 28th, 1852; 6th, Louisa,
b. July 14th, 1854; 7th, Marion, b. July 8th, 1857. 3d, N.
Herman Shattuck, b. June 6th, 1852, m. September 17th, 1845,
Charlotte Ann Crozier of Townsend, and have had, 1st, Ella M.,
b. March 26th, 1851, d. September 6th, 1852; 2d, Gardner
W., b. January 16th, 1853; 3d, Herbert L., b. March 26th,
1855; 4th, Alice M., b. May 21st, 1862. 4th, Louisa O.
Shattuck, b November 11th, 1827, m. Pillsbury Hodgkins of
Stockton, California, July 28th, 1858, and have, 1st, Sarah
Jane, b. June 4th, 1859, d. June 2d, 1860; 2d, Thos. Gardner,
b. June, 1860; 3d, Willie Mayo, b. December, 1862; 4th,
Lincoln Grant, b. February, 1866. 5th, Mary H. Shattuck, b.
February 14th, 1832, d. August 20th, 1833.

5. Rebecca Shattuck, b. May 11th, 1797, m. April 29th,
1824, Lemuel Hall of Brookline, N. H. He was b. November
17th, 1796, they have had, 1st, Rebecca Jane, b. June 16th,
1826, m. Warren S. Wood of Pepperell, and d. November 23d,
1850, and had, 1st, W. Cornelius; 2d, Georgia J. d. 2d, J.
Henry Hall, b. August 11th, 1827, m. Sarah E. Lawrence of
Pepperell, and have, 1st, Lura E.; 2d, Lillie. 3d, Lemuel F.
Hall, b. July 16th, 1829, m. Rosetta Bliss of Chicopee where
they now reside. 4th, John B. Hall, b. July 12th, 1832, m.
Hannah Shattuck of Lunenburg. 5th, Harvey M. Hall, b.
May 18th, 1836, m. Lucinda Patch of Hollis, N. H. He d.

September 1st, 1864, in the Carver Hospital in Washington, D. C., and have Arthur H. 6th, Emma II. Hall, b. October 27th, 1838. 7th, Clara Ann Hall, b. October 20th, 1840, m. Isaac C. Coggin of California.

6. Olive Shattuck, b. July 8th, 1799, m. May 28th, 1818, Bryant Lawrence of Pepperell. He was b. April 22d, 1795, and d. April 18th, 1822. She d. February 3d, 1849 ; they had, Bryant, b. February 19th, 1822, d. June 5th, 1822.

7. Abel Shattuck, b. July 24th, 1802, m.,1st Mar. 15th, '27, Deverd Verder, b. April 17th, 1798, and d. in Brookline, N. II., October 30th, 1840. He m. 2d, May 10th, 1842, Sally Burnham of Wilton, N. II., b. September 24th, 1799 ; had by his first wife, 1st, Mary E. Shattuck, b. December 5th, 1827, m. June 3d, 1846, Wm. II. Mention of Pepperell, and had, 1st, Mary E., b. October 23d, 1849, d. September, 1864; 2d, Henry E. She d. May. 13th, 1863. 2d, Abel K. Shattuck, b. November 21st, 1829, m. Mary C. Nutting of Pepperell, b. July 24th, 1834 ; they have, Mary Sophia and Harriet Maria, twins.

8. Mary Shattuck, b. Aug. 23d, 1804, (unmarried) in Pepperell ; left arm ground in a cider mill when six years old, and taken off above the elbow.

THE DESCENDANTS OF ABRAHAM BALL OF ATHENS, Vt., BY DELIVERANCE PERHAM.

I. Abraham Ball, 2d, b. Oct. 17th, 1786, m. Dec. 1807, Hannah Edwards of Athens, b. Sept. 17th, 1788, and d. Oct. 8th, 1839. He d. April 17th, 1847. He m., 2d, Nancy Wilson, August, 1840. He had by Hannah E., 1st, Amos T. Ball, b. Sept. 4th, 1808, m. Dec. 26th, 1833, E. R. Harlow, b. June 26th, 1808, d. Sept. 4th, 1840, and had, 1st, Mary C. Ball, b. March 9th, 1835, m. Sept. 23d, 1859, A. A. Shumway. She d. Jan. 20th, 1861. 2d, Margarette D. Ball, b. Sept. 15th, 1836, d. Dec. 20th, 1849. 3d, Nelson II. Ball, b. July 1st, 1838. 4th, Jane M. Ball, b. April 7th, 1840, m. 2d, Roxana Whitney, May 27th, 1841, b. Nov. 11th, 1809, and have, 1st, Sarah E. Ball, b. April 11th, 1847; 2d, Ida A. Ball, b. July 22d, 1849; 3d, Flora J. Ball, b. June 1st, 1851.

3

2. Aaron W. Ball b. Jan. 20th, 1810, m. May 26th, 1839, Ann W. Edwards, b. Nov. 2d, 1810, and have, 1st, Clark W. Ball, b. July 26th, 1835, m. Jan. 1st, 1859, Sarah F. Sanford; 2d, Colon J. Ball, b. June 21st, 1845; 3d, Joseph R. Ball, b. July 24th, 1847; 4th, Emma H. Ball, b. May 28th, 1850.

3. Abraham E. Ball, b. Sept. 21st, 1811.

4. Thomas B. Ball, b. Feb. 19th, 1813; was overseer in a cotton factory at Nashua, N. H.; was caught in a belt and killed instantly July 11th, 1839.

5. Sylvanus M. Ball, b. Jan. 23d, 1815, m. Nov. 26th, 1839, Lucia M. Nichols and has, 1st, Ellen M. Ball, b. Oct. 5th, 1840; 2d, Orrie, b. July 15th, 1847; 3d, Willis Ball, b. Nov. 2d, 1852.

6. Hannah E. Ball, b. Sept. 18th, 1816.

7. James P. Ball, b. July 29th, 1818, d. Dec. 8th, 1840.

8. Timothy H. Ball, b. August 3d, 1820.

9. Joseph R. Ball, b. June 20th, 1822, d. Jan. 6th, 1846.

10. Robert R. Ball, b. July 1st, 1824.

11. Julia A. Ball, b. August 19th, 1826.

12. Franklin P. Ball, b. May 2d, 1828, m. May 23d, 1852, Margaret L. Wilson, b. March 21st, 1824, d. Jan. 2d, 1855; m. 2d, July 21st, 1857, Elizabeth Meachum, b. Sept. 7th, 1834, and have, 1st, twin daughters, b. and d. Feb., 1858; 2d, Maggie E. Ball, b. July 3d, 1861; 3d, George F. Ball, b. Aug. 10th, 1863; 4th, Everett M. Ball, b. Dec. 15th, 1864.

13. Orlando S. Ball, b. Dec. 22d, 1830.

14. Noah J. Ball, b. Sept. 25th, 1835.

II. Deliverance Ball, b. Jan. 11th, 1784, d. March 28th 1849.

III. Hannah Ball, b. July 4th, 1791, m. March 11th, 1812, Samuel Edwards of Athens. She d. Sept. 4th, 1847; they have, 1st, Noah B. 2d, Mary, 3d, Austin, 4th, Joel, 5th, Phineas, 6th, Melinda, 7th, Lovina, 8th, Lorenzo D., 9th, Ann.

IV. Phineas Ball, b. June 16th, 1794, m. August 15th, 1813, Abigail Powers of Athens. He d. Sept. 11th, 1828. She d. 1858; they had, 1st, Dusten C. Ball, b. Dec. 17th. 1814, m. Sept., 24th, 1840, Lucy Ann Perham of Athens. She was b. Oct. 20th, 1816, and had children. 2d, Abigail P. Ball, b. Dec. 5th, 1816, m. —— Powers of Athens.

V. Rebecca Ball, b. Feb. 14th, 1797, m. Oct. 25th, 1813, Abraham Powers of Athens. She d. Feb. 15th, 1830; they had, 1st, Stephen R. Powers, b. Oct. 5th, 1816; 2d, Joseph, M. Powers, b. Oct. 29th, 1818. 3d, Olive Powers, b. Jan. 5th, 1825.

VI. Olive Ball, b. June 1st, 1799, m. Feb. 8th, 1818, Samuel S. Stearns. She d. August 28th, 1831, and had, 1st, Philena Stearns, 2d, Ebenezer Stearns, 3d, Harriet Stearns, 4th, Nathaniel Stearns, 5th, Hannah Stearns.

VII. Ebenezer Ball, b. July 29th, 1802, d. Aug. 23d, 1822.

VIII. Noah Ball, b. Mar. 3d. 1805, d. March 4th, 1805.

IX. Mark Ball, b. April 15th, 1806, m. Oct. 5th, 1842, Elizabeth Deputron of Athens, and has, 1st, Curtis M. Ball, b. July 8th, 1843; 2d, Martha Jane Ball, b. August 10th, 1847; 3d, Charlie E. Ball, b. Nov. 17th, 1852; 4th, Clara B. Ball, b. Oct. 24th, 1858.

DESCENDANTS OF BATHSHEBA BALL, BY HEZEKIAH WINN.

I. Polly Winn, b. April 22d, 1792, m. Jan. 20th 1814, Rogers Weston of Mason, N. H. He was b. Apr. 11th, 1789, d. May 11th, 1862; they have 1st, Walter Weston, b. Jan. 7th, 1815, m. Sept 10th, 1844, Lucy Winship of Mason, N. H.; m. 2d, March 23d, 1864, Elmira Morse of Mason. They had, 1st, Lucie A.; 2d, Abbie M. 2. Sumner J. Weston, b. July 18th, 1816, m. July 12th, 1846, Sarah Morse of Mason; they have, 1st, Arvena; 2d, Adah; 3d, Charles A.; 4th, Frank; 5th, Freddie R. 3. Mary Weston, b. May 10th, 1818, m. Feb. 11th, 1847, John P. French; no issue. 4. Charles Weston, b. June 5th, 1822, m. Oct. 16th, 1849, Julia Roberts of Ashby, Mass.; they had Mary Ella; he d.

II. Joseph Winn, b. Aug. 11th, 1793, m. 1814, Catherine Gassett of Townsend, she was b. Sept. 8th, 1795, d. Dec. 23d, 1863; they had, 1st, Caroline Winn, b. Mar. 18th, 1815, m. Wm. Tyler of Leominster, they had 1st, Geo.; 2d, Milo. 2. Converse Winn, b. March 21, 1816, m. Charlotte A. Bayley, and had, 1st, Chas. C., d Nov. 1863; 2d, Ellen F.; 3d, Herman, d. 3. Eliphus Winn, b. July 21st, 1817, m. Jane A. Wheaton, of Wisconsin; they had, Andrew M., Rebecca D., Catherine. 4. Jane Winn,

b. April 25th, 1819, m. George Weston of Groton; they have Abbie J., and Edward J.; she d. June, 1853. 5. Joseph Winn, 2d., b. Sept 7th, 1820, m. Margaret Eaton of Hebron, N. Y. 6. Eliza Winn, b. Feb. 5th, 1822, m. Walter Blood of Townsend; she had Andrew J. Shattuck, b. June 24th, 1839. 7. Geo. Winn, b. May 14th, 1823. 8. Nancy Winn, born Feb. 15th, 1825. 9. Merrill Winn, b. Oct. 29th, 1826, d. Sept 3d, 1844. 10. Osborn Winn, b. July 23d, 1828; he m. and had children and lives in Adamsville, N. Y. 11. Mary A. Winn, b. Aug. 6th, 1831, m. Sherman Howard of Stoddard, N. H.; they had Charles S., Jenney, Clara, Eleanor L. 12. Sumner Winn, b. Aug. 27th, 1833, d. Jan. 11th, 1854.

III. Rebecca Winn, b. March 21st, 1795, m. Aug. 16th, 1818, Aaron Farrington of Franklin, Mass. He d. Feb. 7th, 1841, aged 51; they had, 1st, Eliza Adaline, b. Aug. 13th, 1819, m. Oct. 13th, 1847, Wm. H. Thomson of Wrentham, and now lives in Hopkinton, and has four children. 2d, Orin Gardner, b. May 31st, 1821, m. Jan. 9th, 1849, Sarah J. Velie, of Butler, Wayne Co., N. Y.; had two children. 3d, Nelson Winn, b. April 22d, 1823, d. Oct 22d, 1854. 4th, Charles Hezekiah, b. April 3d, 1825, m. March. 26th, 1846, Adeline M. Sylvester of Bellingham; has three children. 5th, Susan Maria, b. May 28th, 1827, d. May 15th, 1852. 6th, Permelia Ann, b. Oct. 22th, 1830, m. Jan. 1st, 1854, John H. Eaton of Boston, now lives in Bellingham.

IV. Nancy Winn, b. March 7th, 1797, m. 1823 or 1824, Noah Wallace of Greenbush, N. Y.; they had Amanda, Wm., Henry, Harriet. Parents both dead.

V. Norah Winn, b. March 4th, 1799, m. April 23d, 1816, Deborah V. Wallace of Townsend, b. March 16th, 1797. He d. Jan 18th, 1834; they had Isaac W. Winn, b. June 24th, 1817, m. 1st, Mary Sniffins, m. 2d, Amanda Nickols, N. Y. 2. Susan W. Winn, b. May 19th, 1819, d. Nov. 10th, 1825. 3. James V. Winn, b. Nov. 21st, 1821, m. Lois Palmer. 4. Noah Winn, b. June 28th, 1824, d. Nov. 2d, 1825. 5. Nancy M. Winn, b. March 28th, 1827. 6. Susan E. Winn, b. Nov. 22d, 1829, d. Dec. 3d, 1833. 7. Noah F. Winn, b.

Nov. 7th 1832, m. July 9th, 1861, Tryphena Holman of Lunenburg, b, Nov. 10th, 1833.

VI. Betsy Winn, b. Sept. 8th, 1801, m. Nov. 10th, 1824, Jas. Weston of Mason, N. H., m. 2d,♀J. D. Hildreth, Mar. 10th, 1832, died Dec. 16th, 1865, and had Eliza Jane Weston, b. Aug. 16th, 1825, m. C. Johnson. 1st, Nelson I. Hildreth, b. Aug. 13th, 1833. 2d, George, b. Jan 22d, 1836. 3d, Chas. H., b. Nov. 5th, 1837. 4th, John, born June 2d, 1839. 5th, Hernietta S., born July 12th, 1841, died May 5th, 1863. 6th, Sarah A., b. April 23d, 1844. 7th, Georgia A., b. June 23d, 1846. Nelson has Charles H., Freddie A., Effa A., Everett, d. Feb. 11th, 1861.

VII. Hannah Winn. b. July 20th, 1805, m. March 1st, 1832, Eli Boynton of Pepperell, b. April 21st, 1806, d. Nov. 18th, 1861; she d. May 8th, 1856, and had, 1st, Maria B., b. April, 1835 ; 2d, John E., b. Dec. 28th, 1836 ; 3d, Martin L., b. Sept., 1840.

VIII. Sylvia Winn, b. Aug. 4th, 1807, m. Sept. 1827, Nathan Hawes, of Franklin, Mass., and had, 1st, Lewis W. Hawes, b. Oct. 16th, 1828, m. Oct. 22d, 1860, Vienna Scars of Portland, Ct. He d. Feb. 25th, 1866. 2d, Mary Jane Hawes, b. Aug. 8th, 1832. 3d, Nancy Maria Hawes, b. Oct. 22d, 1835.

DESCENDANTS OF NOAH BALL BY BETSY WESTON.

I. Betsy Ball, b. July 26th, 1798, d. Nov. 6th, 1800, aged 2 years.

II. Susan Ball, b. April 29th, 1800, d. Sept. 4th, 1803, aged 3 years.

III. Noah Ball, b. July 23th, 1802, m. Sept. 16th, 1830, Huldah Tenney of Pepperell, b. Jan. 25th, 1813, and have, 1st, Elizabeth M. Ball, b. Sept. 9th, 1832, m. May 7th, 1851, Wm. J. Smith of Brookline, N. H. She d. May 22d, 1863 ; they had, 1st, Charles W. Smith, b. Dec. 8th, 1854 ; 2d, Lizzie E., b. April 11th, 1863, d. Sept. 16th, 1863. 2d, Julia A. E.

Ball, b. Dec. 6th, 1842. 3d, Eliel S. Ball, b. March 27th, 1848.

IV. Melinda Ball, b. Nov. 27th, 1804, m. 1st, June, 26th, 1828, Solomon Jewett of Townsend, b, Jan 26th, 1795, and d. Aug. 26th, 1833 ; m. 2d, June 6th, 1838, Earl Tenney of Pepperell, b. March 11th, 1808; he d. April 24th, 1839, m. 3d, Dec. 30th, 1839, Asa Walker of Ashby, b. Feb. 14th, 1805, and had Joanna M. E., b. May 13th, 1849, d. Aug. 8th, 1850.

V. Flint Ball, b. May 5th, 1807 ; m. May 9th, 1833, Lucy Spaulding of Townsend, b. Feb. 20th, 1812, and had 1st, Walter J. Ball, b. April 7th, 1834 ; 2d, Eliel S. Ball, b. July 21st, 1841, and d. Feb. 28th, 1842. 3d, Charles E. Ball, b. Feb. 20th, 1843, and d. in the army, June 29th, 1863.

VI. Walter Ball, b. Aug. 31st, 1809, d. Sept. 17th, 1825, aged 16.

VII. Lucy Eliza Ball, b. Oct. 14th, 1811, m. Oct. 1833, Eliel Shumway of Oxford, Mass., b. 1809; she d. Dec. 1st, 1864.

VIII. Ralph Ball, b. Feb. 1st, 1814, m. May 8th, 1836, Susan Spaulding of Townsend, b. Nov. 26th, 1814, and had 1st, Oren S. Ball, b. Sept. 25th, 1840. 2d, Noah H. Ball, b. Feb, 16th, 1846, d. Nov. 28th, 1848.

IX. Emily Ball, b. Feb. 9th, 1817, d. Sept. 7th, 1825.

DESCENDANTS OF MARY BALL, BY ZACCHEUS RICHARDSON.

I. Zaccheus Richardson, b. April 12th, 1800, m. May 13th, 1821, Eliza Fisher of Bolton, b. March 4th, 1804, and had 1st, Geo. W. Richardson, b. March 16th, 1822, m. Susan J. Sheldon of Adams. 2d, Jerome F. Richardson, b. June 1st, 1833, m. Mary Fowler. 3d, Mary Ann Richardson, b. Oct. 31st, 1825, m. Byam Spaulding of Chelmsford. 4th, Levi H. Richardson, b. Jan. 25th, 1827, m. Jane Green of Lunenburg. 5th, James Richardson, b. Sept. 23d, 1831, m. H. G. Wheeler of New Ipswich, N. H. 6th, Albert Richardson, b. Aug. 13th, 1834,

m. Julia Heywood of Chelmsford, b. Dec. 7th, 1834 ; settled in Cal., and has two children. 7th, Amos Richardson, b. April 26th, 1836. 8th, Alva Richardson, b. Jan. 25th, 1838.

II. Uzza Richardson, b. Sept. 5th, 1801, d. Oct. 1st, 1812.

III. Mary Richardson, b. Jan. 4th, 1804, d. July 10th, 1836.

IV. Levi Richardson, b. Dec. 11th, 1805, m. Feb. 2d, 1832, Nancy P. Adams of Townsend, b. Aug. 14th, 1809, and has, 1st, Elizabeth A. Richardson, b. Oct. 12th, 1832, m. Jan. 28th, 1851, B. F. King of Leominster, b. 1831, and has Mary E., Joseph J., Alfred R. 2d, Mary B. Richardson, b. Jan. 21st, 1837, d. 1865, with the small pox. 3d, Lucy P. Richardson, b. Feb. 1839. 4th, Edson A. Richardson, b. Feb. 22d, 1841, d. May 6th, 1863, in the war. 5th, Lydia Ann Richardson, b. March 4th, 1845. 6th, Nancy J. Richardson, b. Sept. 23d, 1849. 7th, Levi R. Richardson, b. Aug. 8th, 1851.

V. Esther Richardson, b. Nov. 9th, 1807, m. Feb. 29th, 1833, Benjamin Heywood of Chelmsford. For children see B. Heywood family.

VI. David Richardson, b. Aug. 17th, 1809, m. Oct. 1st, 1838, Maria Smith, she was b. July 16th, 1806, settled in Fitchburg, no issue.

VII. Rebecca Richardson, b. May 18th, 1813, m. Dec. 29th, 1835, John Bryant of Lynnfield, b. May 3d, 1810, they have, 1st, John W. Bryant b. Oct. 9th, 1836, m. June 5th, 1861, Cynthia A. Nelson, b. Aug. 5th, 1836, at Monroe, N. H. ; they have, 1st, John V., 2d, Laura. 2d, Albert R. Bryant, b. June 25th, 1842, m. June 29th, 1865, Sarah E. Danforth of Lynnfield, b. Oct. 4th, 1843.

VIII. Uzza Richardson, b. Sept. 18th, 1814, d. June 15th, 1844.

ANOTHER BRANCH OF THE BALL FAMILY.

Lieut. Jeremiah Ball, son of Jeremiah Ball, who came from Concord to Townsend, and brother of Ebenezer Ball, who settled near the old homestead, was b. August 31st, 1731, m. Mary Stephens, Jan. 1759, and d. March 7th, 1792 ; she was b. March 11th, 1739, d. May 3d, 1825, they had 11 children. 1st, Mary b. Jan. 31st, 1760. m. Daniel Brown of Ashby, Mass. 2d, Jeremiah, b. Feb. 2d, 1762, m. Lucy Putnam of Townsend, d. Oct. 15th, 1813, she was b. Feb. 23th, 1771, d. May 9th, 1805, m. 2d, Sally Haynes of Townsend, b. March 20th, 1782, d. Jan. 17th, 1852. 3d, Jas. b. Jan. 1st, 1764, m. Rebecca Shattuck of Pepperell, Nov. 17th, 1791, and d. Aug. 15th, 1850. She was b. Jan. 23th, 1769, and d. Feb. 8th, 1829. 4th, Betsy b. March 10th, 1768. 5th, John b. May 12th, 1771. 6th, David b. Aug. 25th 1773. 7th, Joseph b. Nov. 14th, 1775. 8th, Daniel b. Sept. 22d, 1778. 9th, Samuel b. Feb. 13th, 1781. 10th, Sarah b. Aug. 31st, 1785. 11th, John b. May 2d, 1790. d.

MARY BALL'S CHILDREN BY DANIEL BROWN.

1st, Joseph m. Maria Hunt of Rindge, N. H., 1823. 2d, Mary. 3d, Daniel, m. Sally Fletcher of New Ipswich, N. H. 4th, Ephraim, lives in Salem, Mass.

The above Joseph Brown, D. D., preached to the seamen in Charleston, S. C., for several years, under the patronage of the Sailor's Friend Society, and was afterwards elected Secretary of said society, and removed to the city of New York.

CHILDREN OF JEREMIAH BALL, BY LUCY PUTNAM & S. HAYNES.

Lucy b. Dec. 26th, 1798, m. Dennis Howe of Ringe, N. H., Dec. 8th, 1825 ; he was b. Feb. 28th, 1800.

Submit, also a twin, b. May 3d, 1805. Mary, daughter of Sally Haynes, b. April 21st, 1810, m. Joseph Kendall of Ashby, Mass., Nov. 23d, 1830 ; he was b. Dec. 24th, 1805.

JAMES BALL'S CHILDREN, BY REBECCA SHATTUCK.

James D., b. Jan. 28th, 1794, m. Mary Farnsworth. John Ball, b. June 15th, 1796, m. Rebecca Proctor, Feb 3d, 1818. Nehemiah b. Sept. 3d, 1798. David, b. Nov. 20th, 1804, m. Julia West, settled in Oregon Territory. Jonas, b. July 3d, 1807, m. Roxa Nichols of Haverhill, Mass., d. Aug. 14th, 1850. Sarah, b. April 18th, 1810, m. Benjamin Mead of Swansey, N. II., March 7th, 1833.

MARY BALL'S GRAND CHILDREN.

Joseph Brown, son of J. Brown, S. Almira, A. Mariah, Charles F., children of D. Brown.

JEREMIAH BALL'S GRAND CHILDREN.

Fanny W. Howe, b. Dec. 1st, 1826. Andrew Howe, b. Dec. 9th, 1828. Walter H. Howe, b. March 14th, 1830, d. Feb. 23d, 1858. Andrew K. Howe, b. June 17th, 1832, d. May 23d, 1838. Sylvanus W. Howe, b. May 20th, 1834, d. Oct. 6th, 1853. Ellen R. Howe, b. April 15th, 1836, d..June 21st, 1838. Milton S. Howe, b. May 4th, 1838, d. Nov. 24th, 1862. Ann E. Howe, b. June 23d, 1840, m. Amos J. Blake, of Fitzwilliam, N. H., Dec. 26th, 1865. Gilman D. Kendall, b. July 4th, 1831, d. July 7th, 1831. Ellen M. Kendall, b. Aug. 9th, 1833, d. Dec. 27th, 1834. Albert W. Kendall, b. Dec. 18th, 1834, d. Feb. 20th, 1863. Henry M. Kendall, b. May 7th, 1837, d. Jan. 14th, 1843, John F. Kendall, b. Sept. 11th, 1839, m. Mary Potter.

JAMES BALL'S GRAND CHILDREN.

Arvilla Ball, Saphrona Ball, Mary Ann Ball, Harriet Ball, children of James Ball. 2d, Dexter Ball, b. Dec. 31st, 1818, m. Jan. 1st, 1840; Nehemiah Ball, b. Feb 1st, 1823, m. Sept

22d, 1847, d. Nov. 6th, 1653; Worcester H. Ball, b. Oct 30th, 1825, m. Oct. 21st, 1848; Rosanna Ball, b. Oct. 1st, 1827, m. May 12, 1846, d. Jan. 10th, 1853; Allen W. Ball, b. July 25th, 1829, m.[Dec. 28th, 1853, d. Jan. 30th, 1867; Henry M. Ball, b. April 13th, 1831, m. Oct. 13th, 1852, and d. Jan. 11th, 1863; Rebecca Ball, b. April 1st, 1834, m. Nov. 21st, 1857, d. Nov. 21, 1858, children of John Ball. Milton Ball, Emma J. Ball, Harvey L. Ball, Julia Ann Ball, Geo. F. Ball, Calvin Ball, Joseph L. Ball, Albert E. Ball, children of David Ball. Sarah Jane Ball, Frances Ball, John N. Ball, children of Jonas Ball. Laura A. Mead, b. Oct. 21st, 1837, m. Jan. 14th, 1858, d. July 10th, 1865. Benjamin F. Mead, b. Oct. 15th, 1832, m. Sept. 1st, 1861, Sarah Ball's children.

The Westons came to this country from Buckinghamshire, England, about the year 1640, settled in Salem, Mass. We find but an imperfect history of them for several generations after their arrival in this country.

John Weston, b. in England, m. Sarah Fitch, April 18th, 1653; they had eight children. Their fourth child, John, was born March 9th, 1661. He was m. to Mary Bryant, Nov. 26th, 1684, and had fourteen children. Samuel, their third child, was born July 16th, 1689. He married Joanna Upham, who died Feb. 26, 1771. Their children were, 1st, Samuel, b. Apr. 16th, 1722, m. Sarah Rogers, d. Oct 5th, 1772. 2d, Sarah, b. Nov. 26th, 1728, m. Lemuel Jinkins. 3d, Jonathan, b. April 13th, 1731, m. Martha Farnsworth. 4th, Joanna b. Feb. 9th, 1744, m. John Weston, d. Oct. 12th, 1775; settled in Reading. Samuel Weston, m. Sarah Rogers, 1743. He removed to Townsend in 1768, to the old fort built for protection against the Indians. Their children were, 1st, William, b. Feb. 9th, 1744, in Billerica, m. Dec. 9th, 1768, Rebecca F. Eaton of Reading, Mass., d. Oct. 15th, 1819, at Townsend. 2d, Sarah, b. Aug. 11th, 1745, d. Oct 16th, 1749, in Townsend. 3d, Sarah b. July 7th, 1747, d. Nov. 18th, 1749, in Townsend. 4th, Abigail b. Nov. 28th, 1749, d. June 4th, 1790, in Townsend. 5th, Sarah, b. April 3d, 1752, in Billerica, m. Timothy Emerson, 1785, and d. June, 1820, in Ashby. 6th, Samuel, b. Oct. 22d, 1754, in Billerica, d. Oct. 27th, 1775, in Townsend. Wounded in the knee at the battle of Bunker Hill; died of the camp fever. 7th, Rogers, b. Sept. 30th, 1757, in Billerica, m. 1st,

Deborah Lawrence, April 12th, 1785; m. 2d, Anna Frost, Dec. 1799; she d. April 30th, 1829; m. 3d, Rebecca Keyes, April 27th, 1830; she d. Aug. 15th, 1830. Her maiden name was Rebecca Ball, who was the 2d wife of his brother Wm., and sister to Noah Ball, who m. Betsey, daughter of Wm. Weston: He m. 4th, Lydia Buttrick, 1831 ; she d, May 18th, 1837. He m. 5th, Betsey Wright, Sept. 1837. He was a prominent man in the affairs of the town, and represented the town five years in the Legislature. He died March 9th, 1843, in Mason, N. H. 8th, Mary b. Oct. 5th, 1759, in Billerica, d. Aug. 1st, 1774, in Townsend. 9th, John b. June 23d, 1762, in Billerica, d. Feb. 29th, 1764, in Townsend. 10th, Joanna, b. Sept. 19th, 1764, Billerica, m. Asa Walker, Sept. 21st, 1796, d. Nov. 13th, 1842, in Ashby. 11th, Phebe, b. Dec. 19th, 1766, m. Ebenezer Ball, Oct, 10th, 1787, d. Nov. 2d, 1848, in Townsend. 12th, Azubah, b. Oct. 4th, 1769, in Townsend, m. Aaron Felt, Jan. 25th, 1791, d. Aug. 18th, 1837, in Temple, N. H.

Wm. Weston, m. Mrs, Rebecca Flint Eaton, Dec. 9th, 1768, (she had one son, Wm. Eaton, by her former marriage.) Wm. Weston came to Townsend with his father and settled with him on the same farm. His children by Rebecca F. Eaton, were, 1st, Thomas b. Sept. 25th, 1769, m. Mercy Cary, of Lyme, N. H., June 3d, 1796; he d. Aug. 10th, 1836, in Springfield, Ohio. 2d, John, b. Aug. 3d, 1771, m. Hannah Chace, Londonderry, N.H., in 1796, d. at Westport, N.Y. 3d, Rebecca, b. Nov. 8th, 1773, m. David Locke, of Ashby, Mass., May 23d, 1796, d. Oct. 31st, 1851, in Ashby. 4th, Betsey, b. Feb. 29th, 1776, m. Noah Ball, of Townsend, May 26th, 1796 ; she d. Sept 16th, 1843, in Townsend. 5th, Sam'l, b. Sept. 7th, 1777, m. 1st, Hannah Parker, of Chelmsford, in 1800, m. 2d, Mary Dunlap, in 1825 ; he d. Dec. 10th, 1836, in Antrim, N.H. 6th, Mary, b. Oct. 21st, 1779, m. Daniel Fuller, of Lyme, N. H., in 1800, m. 2d, Amos Herrick, of Mason, N. H., and d. Dec. 18th, 1863. 7th, Eunice, b. Sept. 8th, 1781, m. Levi Richardson, of Londonderry, Vt.

Wm. Weston, m. for his second wife, Rebecca Ball, Feb. 20th,

1787. Their children were, 1st, Lucy, b. March 11th, 1789, m. Samuel Rockwood, of Groton, March, 1810 ; she d. April, 1843, in Groton. 2d, William, b. March 1st, 1791, m. Dolly Hodgman, of Ashby, Oct. 24th, 1816, d. Aug. 18th, 1866, in Townsend. 3d, Sarah b. Sept. 18th 1794, m. John Hodgman, of Townsend, May 9th, 1820, and d. Dec.ˑ10th, 1838, in Townsend.

Wm. WESTON, 2d's CHILDREN BY DOLLY HODGMAN.

1st, Clarissa, b. Mar. 6th, 1818, d. Sept. 28th, 1819. 2d, Charles, b. June 8th, 1819, d. July 15th, 1858. Harriet, b. Oct. 27th, 1822, m. Nero Sherwin, April 1st, 1841. 4th, Wm. 3d, b. Jan. 4th, 1825, m. Harriet Emery, of Lunenburg, Nov. 30th, 1848, and have Lizzie Maria, b. Aug. 22d, 1850.

The following are the names of the Balls and Westons of our connections who lost their lives in the service of their country, to sustain our rights and liberties.

Charles E. Ball son of Flint Ball, and grandson of Noah Ball, of Townsend, enlisted in Co. F, Fifty-third Regiment, Mass. Vols.; was wounded at the first assault on Port Hudson, and died of his wound, in N. Orleans, June 29th, 1863, aged 20 years. He was a good soldier, and faithful in all the duties of life.

LINES

Addressed to his mother, by Mrs. Phebe Weston Farmer of N. Orleans, La.

Where the dark, damp earth is thickly spread
    With graves, unkept by care,
I found, by the board they placed at his head,
    That the grave of dear Charlie was there.

Foremost, he charged with the valiant band
    Who rushed at their leader's call,
Heedless of all save the word of command,
    "We must scale Port Hudson's walls."

Alas! while the early matin bell
    Was telling the hour for prayer,
Where the carnage was thickest, 'twas there he fell;
    Ah! why did not death meet him there?

Then, his grave had been made on the green hillside,
    With the river winding below;
Not here, where slimy reptiles glide,
    And nought save rank weeds grow.

I searched his grave for some flow'ret fair,
    As a token to soften thy grief,
But a tuft of wild clover was all that grew there,
    So I culled you a simple leaf.

George D. Felt, of Temple, N. H., enlisted in Co. G, Second Regiment, N. H. Vols. He was the first to enlist from Temple and the only one for several months; was engaged in thirteen battles; was wounded at the Second Bull Run fight. He lay on the battle-field eleven days in the rebel lines without care; was then paroled and sent to hospital in Alexandria, Va., where he died of his wound Nov. 6th, 1862, aged 27 years.

Edward W. Felt, of Temple, N. H. enlisted in Co. F, Tenth Regiment, N. H Vols.; died at his father's of chronic diarrhœa

Feb. 8th, 1863, aged 21 years. The two last were sons of Daniel Felt, and grandsons of Azubah Weston Felt, of Temple N. H.

Two sons of Mrs. Sarah Felt Hardy of the State of Michigan, and grandsons of Azubah W Felt, of Temple, N. H.

Elnathan Hodgman, son of Sarah Weston Hodgman of Townsend, Mass., enlisted in Co. E, Eighth Regiment, N. H. Vols.; died of chronic diarrhœa on board a steamer on the Mississippi river, on his way home, Jan. 9th, 1865, aged 38 years. He was buried at Memphis, Tenn.

Milton S Howe, of Rindge, N. H., enlisted in the Fourteenth Regiment, N. H. Vols.; died in Maryland of typhoid fever, Nov. 24th, 1862, aged 24 years.

Albert W. Kendall, of Ashby, Mass., enlisted in Co. G, Fifty-third Regiment, Mass. Vols.; died of typhoid fever in Carrollton, La., Feb. 20th, 1863, aged 29 years. The two last were great grandsons of Jeremiah Ball, 2d.

Edson A. Richardson, son of Levi Richardson, and grandson of Mary Ball Richardson, of Townsend, enlisted in Co. D, Fifty-third Mass. Vols.; d. of chronic diarrhœa, in New Orleans, La., May 6th, 1863, aged 22 years.

Wm. Carey Weston, son of Isaac Weston of Indiana, enlisted in Seventy-third Indiana Vols.; was shot at the first day's fight at Stone River, about the 31st of December, aged 23 years.

Thomas J. Weston, son of Silas Weston, of Springfield, Ohio, enlisted in the One Hundred Thirty-eighth Ohio National Guard; was brought home sick, and died of typhoid fever, Sept. 10th, 1864, aged 24 years.

Charles S. Weston, son of Silas Weston of Springfield, Ohio, enlisted in Thirty-fifth Regiment, O. V. I. and died in Louisville, Ky., March 7th, 1862, aged 19 years. The last three were grandsons of Thomas Weston, formerly of Townsend, Mass.

Ralph Weston, son of Sam'l Weston, and grandson of Rogers Weston, of Mason, N. H., enlisted in Co. G, Thirteenth Regiment, N. H. Vols.; died Mar. 21st, 1863, in hospital near Hampton, Va., aged 39 years.

John Weston, son of Lawrence Weston, and grandson of Rogers Weston of Mason, N. H., enlisted in the Thirty-second Regiment Iowa Vols., and was severely wounded in the chest on the
10th of April, at the battle of Pleasant Hill, La., and died of his
wound May 19th, 1863, aged 24 years.

DESCENDANTS NOW LIVING.

Francis W. Wood, of Townsend, enlisted in Company B, 26th
Mass. Infantry, at Boston, Sept. 14th, 1861; went into camp
Cameron. Left Mass. with the Regt. Nov. 21st, proceeded to Ship
Island, Miss., where he remained through the Winter. Left April
15th, 1862, for New Orleans, and various other places in the South,
for two years and six months, when he re-enlisted, and took a furlough
for home. Returning to the South, joined the army, reported at For-
tress Monroe, and various other places, was in Sheridan's campaign
at the Battle of Cedar Creek, Oct. 19th, 1864, was taken prisoner
and carried to Richmond, and put in Pemberton prison. From there
he was removed to Salisbury, N. C., where he was ushered into one of
those Southern pens, so noted for their inhumanity to our soldiers,
where he froze both feet, and his toes all sloughed off, which will
make him a cripple for life.

Jonas Shattuck, of Pepperell, Mass., was out during the war.
Luther Boynton,   "   "   "   nine months.
Geo. W. Ball, of Chicopee,   "   "   "
Geo. V. Ball, Lunenburg, was out four years, promoted to 2d Lieut.
Chas. H. Hildreth, W. Boylston, time unknown.
Curtis M. Ball, Athens, Vt.   "
Jos. C. Shattuck, Brookline, N. H. "